To our good friend
Marylin Hafner

**A Marc Brown ARTHUR Chapter Book**

# King Arthur

Text by Stephen Krensky
Based on a teleplay by Peter Hirsch

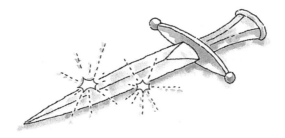

Little, Brown and Company
Boston   New York   London

Text has been reviewed and assigned a reading level by Laurel S. Ernst, M.A., Teachers College, Columbia University, New York, New York; reading specialist, Chappaqua, New York

ISBN 0-316-12178-9 (hc)
ISBN 0-316-12241-6 (pb)
Library of Congress Catalog Card Number 98-67576

10 9 8 7 6 5 4

WOR (hc)
COM-MO (pb)

Printed in the United States of America

# Chapter 1

• • • • • • • • • • •

"Everybody out!" called Mr. Ratburn.

The school bus carrying Arthur's third-grade class had come to a stop at Bear Lake. All around them were colorful tents and knights on horseback, filling the park nearby.

As the students got off the bus, Mr. Ratburn told them to stay together.

"Whoa!" said Arthur, looking around. "This fair is amazing! It's just like being in the Middle Ages."

"Stick with your partner," said Mr. Ratburn. "And take notes on all the historical details. They'll be useful when we compete in the games."

A man dressed as a peasant passed them, pushing a cart.

"Get your haggis here! Fresh haggis! Two for a dollar."

Buster jotted down some notes.

"Haggis. Two . . . for . . . a dollar." He paused. "Hey, what's haggis?"

"Disgusting," said the Brain. "That's all you need to know."

Mr. Ratburn suddenly stopped walking. A look of awe came over his face.

"There it is!" he said. "The Golden Gryphon!"

He pointed to a glass case holding a trophy. The gryphon had the body of a lion, with the head and wings of an eagle.

"This award," Mr. Ratburn explained, "is given to the class that exhibits the greatest knowledge of the Middle Ages."

"Has your class ever won it?" asked Francine.

"No," Mr. Ratburn admitted. "We have not had that pleasure."

Arthur heard the hint of sadness in Mr. Ratburn's voice. He nudged Buster. "Boy," he whispered, "Mr. Ratburn sure wants to win that Golden Gryphon."

"My class came so close to winning last year," said Mr. Ratburn. "If we all try our hardest, I'm sure this year we can come in first."

"Of course we will," Arthur whispered to Buster. "What other class on Earth does as much homework or—"

Arthur stopped speaking, distracted by the sound of marching feet. He turned around as a small platoon of children wearing starchy uniforms approached. They were led by an older man who looked like Robin Hood's father.

"Wow!" said Buster. "I've never seen so

many people dressed like that outside of the army."

"Look at their buttons," said Muffy, who noticed those things. "That's real gold!"

"GLENBROOK, GLENBROOK, THAT'S OUR SCHOOL!" shouted the children crisply. "GLENBROOK, GLENBROOK, WE WILL RULE! GO-O-O-O, GLENBROOK!"

Robin Hood's father raised his hand, and the children came to a halt.

"Ah, Ratburn . . . we meet again!"

Mr. Ratburn looked a little pale, but he still stepped forward to shake hands.

"Good to see you again, Mr. Pryce-Jones."

"Yes, yes, I'm sure it is. You probably thought your old teacher had retired at last." Mr. Pryce-Jones smiled. "But they won't let me quit! After all, I'm irreplaceable."

One of the Glenbrook girls cleared her throat and pointed to a nearby sundial.

"Excuse me, sir, but it's 10:14."

Muffy let out a little gasp. This girl had on a bracelet she had admired at the jewelry store. But her parents had said it was too expensive, even for them.

Mr. Pryce-Jones nodded. "Ah, thank you, Buffy. Well, time to prepare. See you at Merlin's Labyrinth, Ratburn. Don't get lost in the meantime."

He let out a small laugh and led his troop away.

# Chapter 2

Merlin's Labyrinth was a maze with canvas sides stretched between a series of tent poles. There were two entrances to the maze but only one exit. As Mr. Ratburn had explained it, two students would compete against each other to see who could get out first.

A man dressed as Merlin the wizard stood between the two entrances.

"Who dares to invade my sanctuary?" he demanded.

"Me, I guess," said Arthur, who was standing in front of one of the entrances.

"And I, my liege, have come from afar

to pick up your gauntlet as well," said a boy from Glenbrook named Chester.

"Bravely spoken, my lad," said Merlin, gracing Chester with a nod.

Arthur fidgeted. He wished he had thought to say something like that.

Now Merlin raised his arms above his head and spoke sternly:

*"The first to escape, a point shall win.*
*The other one will perish within!"*

"Remember, Chester," said Mr. Pryce-Jones. "Navigate by the sun and the tops of trees! And remember your ball of string."

Chester nodded and checked his pocket.

Mr. Ratburn patted Arthur on the shoulder. "Arthur," he said, "just use your head."

"On your mark!" said Merlin. "Get set! Hie thee hence!"

Chester darted into the maze while Arthur stood blinking in the sunlight.

"That means 'Go!' kid," Merlin explained.

"Oh," said Arthur. Then he entered the maze as well.

He ran down the canvas hallways, turning right, then left, then right again. He had no idea where he was going. He just hoped that if he ran around long enough, he might come upon the exit by accident.

When he came to an intersection, Arthur stopped to catch his breath. He wondered which way to go. But the canvas gave no clues. It all looked the same.

I'll go left, he decided, and started off again. But after taking a few twists and turns, Arthur came to a dead end.

I'd better turn back, he thought.

Then Arthur saw a silhouette standing on the other side of the canvas. At first he thought it might be Chester, but when he

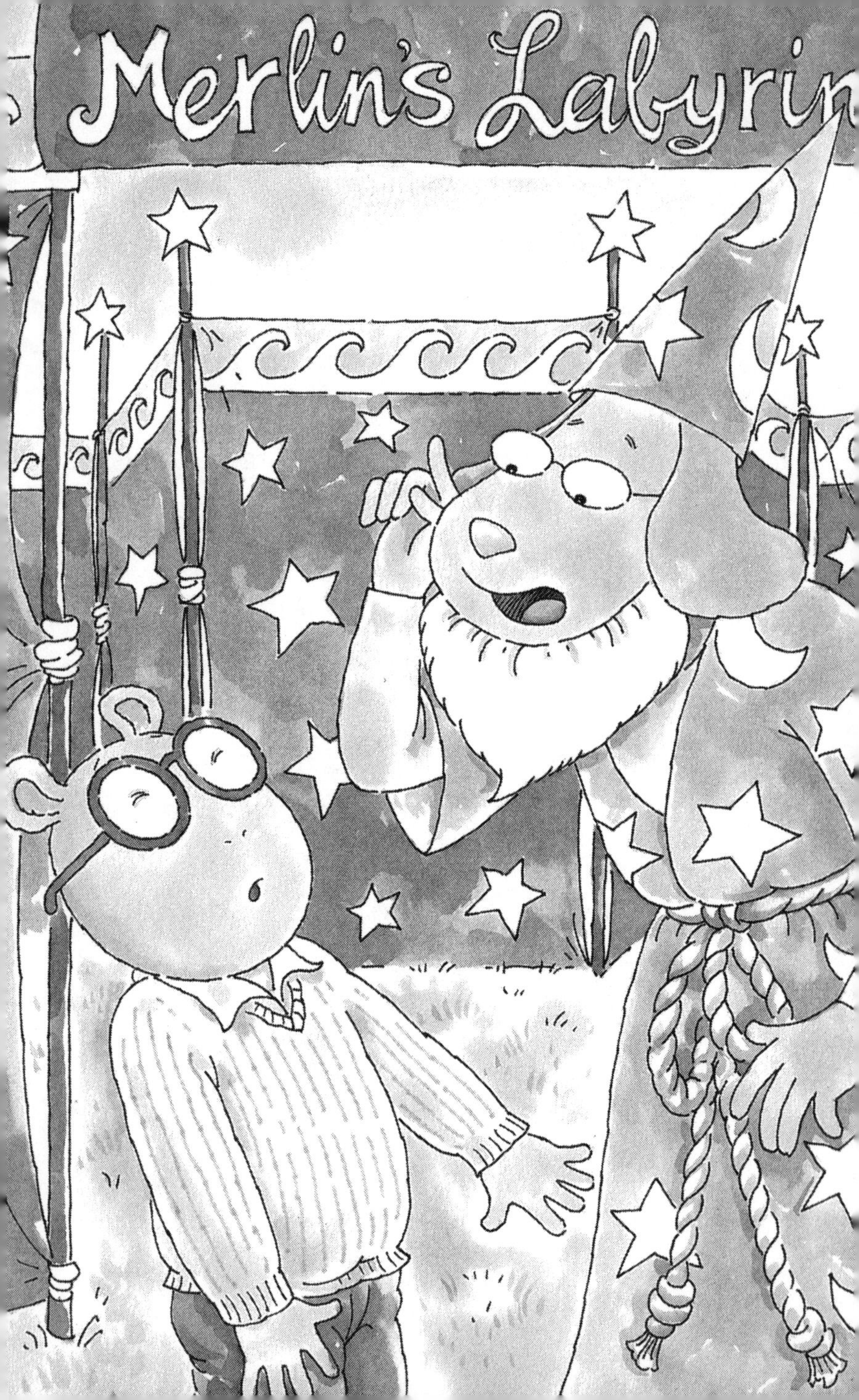
Merlin's Labyrin

raised his hand, the silhouette did the same. He stepped to the right. So did the silhouette. Finally, he scratched his head. The silhouette scratched, too.

Arthur lowered his arm. "Hmmmph! It's just my shadow."

Now, maybe Arthur had simply gotten dizzy from so much running around, but he thought he saw his shadow go on scratching—even though *he* had stopped. Startled, Arthur fell backward and tumbled into one of the canvas walls.

*Rrriiipppppp!*

Arthur burst through the canvas, stumbling out of the side of the maze.

"Guess I really did use my head," he said.

"But that won't help you now," declared Merlin, coming up to inspect the damage. "You, young sir, are disqualified."

At that moment, Chester emerged from the exit.

11

"The winner!" Merlin proclaimed.

Arthur looked back to where the rest of the class was watching. Nobody met his gaze. They were all staring at the ground in disappointment.

# Chapter 3

After the disaster at Merlin's Labyrinth, Arthur felt a little dizzy. While the rest of the class took turns competing, he found a shady spot to sit down.

Arthur felt bad about messing up in the maze, but he told himself it wasn't all his fault. It wasn't like he had a lot of experience with mazes. Arthur remembered the ancient Greek story about Theseus, who found his way out of a maze by unraveling a ball of string behind him.

"But nobody told us to bring any string

today," he muttered. Chester, however, had clearly thought ahead.

A loud groan drew his attention. Just behind some trees, a bunch of kids were lined up in front of a large stone. The stone was about the size of a wheelbarrow. It looked like a perfectly ordinary stone — except for the fact that a sword handle was sticking out of it.

Arthur heard the groan again. It came from the kid who was holding the sword handle. She seemed to be trying to pull it from the stone.

She was not having much luck.

"Next!" said a peasant who was overseeing the girl's efforts.

Arthur walked up to him. "What's this line for?" he asked.

"He or she who pulls the sword from the stone is truly our king or queen. 'Tis an equal opportunity sword."

"That sounds fair," said Arthur.

But the peasant wasn't done speaking:

*"All your might won't set things right.
'Tis a gentle hand 'twill rule the land."*

Arthur waited his turn, watching all the kids ahead of him fail in their attempts. Arthur didn't understand why it should be so hard. If the sword had been put into the stone, surely it could be pulled out the same way.

But when he finally got his chance, he did no better than the rest.

"Uggghhhh!" he groaned.

But the sword didn't move. Arthur wanted to try again, but Francine interrupted him.

"Arthur!" she shouted. "We have to go! It's time for the tug-of-war."

\* \* \*

The Lakewood team and the Glenbrook team stood on opposite sides of a muddy pit. Each side was holding one end of a thick rope. A ribbon had been tied in the middle, and whichever team could grab the ribbon would win the contest.

So far, though, the ribbon had not moved much to either side.

"We must use brains as well as brawn," Mr. Pryce-Jones called out to his team. "Remember the ancient Egyptians building their pyramids, and pay heed to Archimedes!"

The Glenbrookers paused for a moment. Then they pulled sharply together.

"Uh-oh!" cried Arthur as he and the other Lakewooders were yanked forward into the mud.

"The winners!" announced the herald standing by, indicating the Glenbrook team.

Afterward, Mr. Pryce-Jones walked over to Mr. Ratburn, who was picking himself up and wiping dirt from his pants.

"Surely," Mr. Pryce-Jones declared, "you remember Archimedes, who said that with the proper leverage, he could move the world. Apparently, your students haven't learned that yet."

"Apparently not," said Mr. Ratburn thoughtfully. "Apparently not."

# Chapter 4

· · · · · · · · · · · ·

After their group defeat in the tug-of-war, Arthur's classmates entered other contests individually.

Francine competed at archery. Her best shot landed right in the middle of the yellow bull's-eye.

"Try and beat that," she told her opponent, Colleen.

Colleen just smiled.

"I'll do my best," she said.

She licked the end of the suction cup, then fired her arrow. It landed directly above Francine's and then slid down, knocking Francine's arrow off the target.

Francine gasped. "How did you do that?" she said.

Colleen shrugged. "I've seen *The Adventures of Robin Hood* a hundred and thirty-four times. I've picked up a few things along the way."

Muffy wasn't having much better luck on the tennis court. The ball used in the Middle Ages was much heavier than the ones she was used to. When Buffy served to her, the ball knocked Muffy's racket right out of her hand.

"My point!" said Buffy.

Muffy bent down to retrieve her racket. "Where did you learn to play like that?" Muffy asked.

"Oh, King Henry VIII was my great-great-great-great-great-great-great-great-great-uncle. So you see, we've been playing tennis in my family for a *lonnnng* time."

Just before lunch, everyone went down to the lake. Buster lay on a picnic table, looking at the clouds. Francine and Arthur were brushing dried mud off their clothes.

"We're getting pulverized!" said Francine. "We might as well just *give* them the Golden Gryphon."

Arthur sighed. "It's not our fault that we're playing against computerized robots."

"I feel sorry for them," said Buster.

Arthur and Francine looked shocked.

"You do?" said Arthur.

"Why?" asked Francine.

"Because," said Buster, "they have *that* guy for a teacher. A teacher like that would be my worst nightmare."

"You're wrong there, Buster," said Mr. Ratburn, coming up behind them. "Mr.

Pryce-Jones was the best teacher I ever had."

His students were amazed. "Really?" they said together.

"Oh, yes. I remember him well. You know, some people say I'm a tough teacher—"

"No-o-o!" said Buster.

"Who says that?" asked Arthur.

"Yeah, who?" added Francine.

Mr. Ratburn smiled. "Oh, a teacher hears these things. But I'm a softy compared to Mr. Pryce-Jones. Why, when I was in third grade, he made us learn Latin. I still remember conjugating the verb *to be: sum, es, est, sumus, estes, sunt.* Of course, we did more than study," said Mr. Ratburn. "He pushed us at recess, too. The body is a temple, he often said, and we need to honor it by exercising."

"Gee, I've never thought of my body as

a temple," said Francine. She stood up a little straighter.

Mr. Ratburn folded his arms. "I learned a lot. It makes me wonder sometimes if I should be tougher."

Arthur, Francine, and Buster exchanged panicked looks. An even tougher Mr. Ratburn? thought Arthur. Win or lose, they had to keep that from happening.

# Chapter 5

In the medieval banquet tent, both classes were sitting on opposite sides of a long table. Mr. Ratburn sat at one end and Mr. Pryce-Jones at the other.

Lunch was being served.

"One good thing about the Middle Ages," said Buster. "No forks. You get to eat everything with your hands."

"As long as you have an appetite," said Francine, who was just poking at her food.

"I know what you mean," said Muffy. "I'm not feeling very hungry, either."

"Well, if you're not eating," said Buster, "pass your plates down here."

"How can you think about food?" asked Francine. "Aren't you getting a little discouraged?"

Buster nodded. "Of course. My brain is very upset. But for my stomach, it's business as usual. Mmmm. This capon is good. It tastes just like chicken."

The Glenbrookers across the table started to laugh.

"What's so funny?" asked Buster.

"Capon *is* chicken," the Brain whispered to him.

At that moment, Mr. Pryce-Jones stood up and called for everyone's attention.

"I have an extra helping of figgy pudding for the student who can answer this question."

Everyone on the Glenbrook side of the table raised a hand.

"Oh, me, me!"

"Over here, sir!"

"Call on me!"

Their teacher beamed at them. "Commendable enthusiasm, children. But let's give Lakewood first crack at it, shall we?"

The hands dropped. All the Glenbrookers folded their arms and stared across the table.

Even Buster stopped eating under the weight of their stares.

"All right, then," said Mr. Pryce-Jones, "listen closely. Who was the sixteenth king of England?"

Arthur blinked.

Francine frowned.

The Brain just scratched his head.

Buster couldn't even think of a joke to fill the silence.

"Tsk, tsk," said Mr. Pryce-Jones. "I see you haven't taught them the song, Ratburn."

Mr. Ratburn admitted that he hadn't.

"Well, there's no time like the present," said Mr. Pryce-Jones. He took a deep breath and directed his class to sing.

*"Here's a song*
*that's more historical than musical,*
*to teach the kings and queens of England*
*in the order categorical."*

Arthur looked at his watch. Fifteen minutes later, he was still looking at it. The Glenbrookers were just finishing up.

*"Now you know a wondrous thing:*
*All of England's queens and kings!"*

The Glenbrook students all applauded loudly. The clapping startled many of the Lakewooders, who had begun to nod off.

Mr. Pryce-Jones sat down. "I know you don't agree with all of my teaching

methods, Ratburn. But you have to admit they're effective. The fact is, you can't beat us."

Mr. Ratburn sighed. "You may be right, sir."

Arthur poked Buster in the side. "Did you hear that? If we keep losing, Mr. Ratburn may start teaching us like this guy. We have to win something."

"But how?" Buster asked. "You heard Mr. Pryce-Jones. He said we can't beat them."

Arthur was not convinced. He looked over a list of events at the fair. "There must be *something* here we're good at . . ."

His finger moved down the list of events.

"Aha!" he said finally.

It was time to fight back.

# Chapter 6

Buster sat at a long wooden table outside the dining tent. Arthur stood behind him, massaging his shoulders.

"Are you ready, champ?" asked Arthur.

Buster nodded. "A pie-eating contest should be my best event. What kind of pie did you say it was?" he asked, facing the row of pies before him.

"Mincemeat," said Arthur.

"I don't think I've ever tried that. My favorite is blueberry. Well, actually, I like cherry and pumpkin and lemon meringue."

"What about apple?" asked Arthur.

"Can't forget that," Buster agreed. "Not to mention peach, strawberry, rhubarb, pecan, and key lime. So I suppose I won't mind adding mincemeat to the list." He licked his lips. "Good thing I didn't win that figgy pudding."

Next to Buster was a student named Rusty from Glenbrook. He faced an equally long line of pies.

An official dressed as a friar stood at the head of the table.

"Now, you both know the rules. It's really very simple. Whoever eats the most pies wins. Ready? Good. On your mark. Get set. Tuck in!"

Buster immediately grabbed a pie and started shoving it into his mouth, chewing and swallowing as fast as possible. Rusty, in contrast, stopped to put a linen napkin on his lap. Then he began cutting up his first pie with a knife.

"He-wnt-evr-ctch-me-at-tht-rate," mumbled Buster.

"What?" asked Arthur.

Buster swallowed. "I said, he won't ever catch me at that rate."

Time passed. Buster had almost finished three pies. Rusty was at least half a pie behind, but he continued to eat at a steady pace.

"Come on, Buster!" said Arthur. "Keep going!"

Buster held a piece of pie in front of his mouth. It was not the biggest piece he had swallowed. But somehow his mouth seemed unwilling to open.

"Must . . . eat . . . more!" Buster gasped.

But he couldn't. His lips were sealed. Finally, he dropped the pie in disgust.

Rusty, meanwhile, had finished a third pie and was calmly starting a fourth. "How can you just keep going?" Buster asked him. "WHERE DOES IT ALL GO?"

Rusty dabbed at his mouth with his napkin. "Over the past few weeks," he explained, "I've expanded my stomach capacity with larger and larger breakfasts. I now have an eighteen-liter capacity." He turned to the friar. "Would you possibly have any ice cream to go with this?"

Buster groaned.

"Let's go," said Arthur. "You'll feel better after we take a little walk."

He helped Buster up from the table. Buster wasn't able to move very fast, so Arthur just shuffled along beside him. As they stopped to rest for a moment, Arthur recognized a voice talking behind some trees.

It was Lakewood's principal, Mr. Haney.

"After seeing your results, I know the children would benefit from your experience," he said.

"Well," said another voice. It was Mr.

Pryce-Jones. "The offer is certainly gener-
ous. I'll definitely consider it."

Arthur turned pale. "Oh, no!" he muttered. This was the worst news yet.

# Chapter 7

· · · · · · · · · · ·

Francine and Muffy were sitting at a table near the unicorn-dog stand.

Arthur came running up, with Buster following behind him.

"Hey, Arthur!" said Francine. "Try a unicorn-dog. It tastes like chicken."

"Not now," said Arthur. "I've lost my appetite. I just heard Mr. Haney talking with Mr. Pryce-Jones. Mr. Haney offered him a teaching job. I think he's planning to replace Mr. Ratburn."

"It must be because we've lost every single event," said Muffy. "We've disgraced Mr. Ratburn and the school."

Buster sighed. "Mr. Pryce-Jones will probably hold us back for years so he can teach us over and over again."

"Don't give up yet," said Francine. "The Brain is in the next contest. How can we lose?"

The Brain was sitting in a chair on a wooden stage. Sitting across from him was I.Q., a Glenbrook student. Between them was a giant wheel marked with different numbers.

A man dressed as a jester had rattled off many questions to each contestant. So far, neither had made a mistake.

Arthur, Francine, and Buster were watching in the audience.

"You can do it, Brain!" Buster cried. "No one's smarter than you!"

"Time for the tiebreaker," said the jester. He spun the wheel.

*"The Wheel of Fortune, watch it spin!*
*Someone will lose; someone will win!"*

The wheel stopped on the number twenty.

"All right," said the jester, "for twenty points, what do all the planets revolve around?"

"The sun!" said the Brain. He waved to his friends. "That was easy."

"I'm sorry, Mr. Brain," said the jester, "but the correct answer is the Earth. Those points will go to Mr. I.Q."

"Huh?" said the Brain. "But that's wrong!"

I.Q. smiled at him. "You have to give the answers that were thought to be correct during the Middle Ages. Sorry."

The Brain buried his head in his hands.

"That's it," said Buster. "We've lost for

sure now! We might as well get something to eat."

"Eat?" said Francine. "You just had three pies."

"But now I feel empty inside."

"You can go ahead," Arthur told them. "There's something I want to do."

Arthur felt shy as he once again approached the sword in the stone. There were several kids in front of him, but the line moved fast because everyone got frustrated quickly.

"Don't be so stubborn, sword!" said one student.

"Maybe I can scare you out," muttered the next kid in line.

"It must be a trick," moaned another.

When Arthur got his turn, he tried every approach he could think of. He pulled with his left hand. He pulled with his right. He pulled with both hands and a sharp twist. He pulled with no twist at all.

But the sword stayed put.

"Unggghhhh!" cried Arthur. "Why won't you move?"

The peasant in charge watched every effort without making a comment. But as Arthur walked away, he called out:

> *"The wind has might, as does the sea,*
> *But might need not bring victory."*

Arthur didn't even look back. He was in no mood for peasants and their rhyming riddles. He needed to find some way to win.

Otherwise, Mr. Ratburn was doomed.

# Chapter 8

• • • • • • • • • • • •

"We're running out of time," said Arthur.

He was talking with Buster, Francine, and Muffy outside another large tent.

Francine rolled up her sleeves. "The only event left is a castle-building contest. If we win that, maybe Mr. Haney will reconsider."

They went inside the tent, where all of the kids were hard at work. They had many different kinds of building materials at hand, including cardboard, Styrofoam blocks, pipe cleaners, and tongue depressors.

Arthur, Buster, Muffy, and Francine decided to build a castle together.

"That way," said Arthur, "we have the best chance of impressing the judges."

The castle would have four towers, they decided, and each of them would design one.

"In the long history of castles," said Buster, "this one will be unique."

For the next hour, they cut and pasted and punched holes and colored with markers. The castle took shape, spiked with turrets and fortifications. Buster even made a crank out of a paper clip to raise and lower the drawbridge. As a final touch, Francine made a small Lakewood flag to stand on top.

When it was time to show off their work, all four builders stood proudly behind their table. As a judge passed by, Muffy nudged Buster, who turned the crank to lower the drawbridge.

The judge smiled. "Excellent!" he said. "This is certainly a very creative piece of work."

Standing in the background, Mr. Ratburn beamed.

"Very convincing details," continued the judge. "I especially like the alligators sticking their heads out of the moat."

"That was my idea," said Francine.

"Unfortunately, this contest is for the most historically accurate castle," the judge explained. "While yours is certainly magnificent, it hardly follows any one historical style of the Middle Ages. Therefore, I must give the prize to Glenbrook."

He pointed to another table, where a squat, drab — but authentic — castle was sitting. Mr. Pryce-Jones and his students were standing around it.

"Hip, hip hooray!" they shouted.

Mr. Pryce-Jones came forward and inspected the Lakewood castle.

"You see," he said, placing a tape measure against the walls, "these arrow slits are much too wide. As for your little flag that says *Lakewood*, well, it would have had an *e* at the end in Middle English."

Mr. Ratburn, however, came forward to congratulate his group.

"I want you to know that I'm very proud of your efforts today," he said. "And this castle is magnificent. I'm going to have it put on display the moment we get back to school."

"But we didn't win!" Buster protested.

"As far as I'm concerned, you did," said Mr. Ratburn. "This is a first-rate effort. I can't ask more of you than that."

"Poor Mr. Ratburn," Francine whispered. "He doesn't even know he's being replaced."

Muffy shook her head sadly. "I feel so sorry for him," she said.

"Him?" said Buster. "What about us?

My brain hurts just thinking about Mr. Pryce-Jones."

Francine looked around. "Hey! Where did Arthur go?"

"I don't know," said Buster. "He walked off muttering something about 'our only hope left.'"

"I thought we were out of hope," said Muffy.

The others nodded. They thought so, too.

# Chapter 9

Arthur's first reaction when he saw the sword again was relief. After all, someone could have pulled it from the stone since he was last there.

But nobody had. The sword was still there, and so was the line of people waiting to try and remove it.

Arthur noticed that the line held some familiar faces. A bunch of Glenbrookers were there, including Chester, Colleen, and Buffy. Even Mr. Pryce-Jones was waiting for a turn.

"This is the ultimate challenge," he was

telling his students. "To succeed, you must demonstrate both strength and creativity."

The Glenbrook students nodded at his every word.

"Strength."

"Creativity."

"Strength and creativity."

But words alone did not seem to help. They each had a try. Chester tried with one hand held behind his back, Colleen wrapped her thumbs around the hilt, and Buffy tried kicking the sword loose with her feet.

Yet none of them could budge it an inch.

The peasant in charge folded his arms.

*"All your might won't set things right.*
*'Tis a gentle hand 'twill rule the land."*

Arthur remembered that the peasant had said this before. He was sure it must be a clue. He tried to remember what Mr.

Ratburn had told the class about the legend of Camelot. He knew that the Knights of the Round Table had once brought peace and justice to England. But Mr. Ratburn had emphasized that the knights did not succeed through strength alone. Their strength was tempered with kindness and mercy.

Arthur paused. This had to be the "gentle hand" the peasant was speaking of.

"Now I get it," he said, looking to the peasant and bowing slightly.

The peasant met Arthur's gaze—and allowed himself a small smile.

When his turn came, Arthur gently took hold of the sword with his thumb and forefinger.

"There you are, Arthur!" said Francine, with Buster and Muffy arriving behind her. "Why are you trying that sword again?"

"We have to go!" Muffy shouted at him.

Buster, however, saw the look of determination on Arthur's face.

"You can do it, Arthur. I know you can!"

Arthur nodded. He took the sword in both hands. But instead of pulling on it hard, he gently wiggled it. Then, with a long, slow tug, he pulled the sword free. He raised it high in the air, where a beam of sunlight caught the side of the blade.

"Oooooh!" Francine, Buster, and Muffy exclaimed.

The peasant jumped to attention. "Blimey!" he cried. "We have a new king!"

Everyone else grew silent as the peasant knelt before Arthur. As for the new king himself, he was blushing from head to toe.

# Chapter 10

● ● ● ● ● ● ● ● ● ● ● ● ●

A crowd of people, including both classes, surrounded Arthur. Merlin and the court jester came hurrying from other parts of the fair.

"I didn't mean to cause such a fuss," said Arthur. "I just remembered what Mr. Ratburn taught us about Camelot."

Mr. Ratburn cleared his throat. "Thank you, Arthur."

Merlin then took out a golden crown and placed it on Arthur's head.

"Arthur Read," he said, "I hereby proclaim you king of our fair!"

"How did you know my name?" Arthur whispered.

"I'm a wizard," Merlin whispered back. "And wizards know these things."

Mr. Pryce-Jones was shaking his head. "Young Arthur out-thought not only all my students, but me as well. I couldn't budge that sword."

He walked over to shake Mr. Ratburn's hand.

"Congratulations, Ratburn. You taught that boy how to think for himself and how to learn from the lessons of history. That matters more than just facts and figures. If you've taught the others the same way, you haven't turned out half bad."

Mr. Ratburn blushed. His former teacher did not give compliments easily.

Buster tugged at Mr. Haney's sleeve. "Excuse me," he said, "but since Arthur won the crown, you won't have to replace Mr. Ratburn, will you?"

The principal looked down at him. "Replace? Whatever are you talking about, Mr. Baxter? Nobody's replacing Mr. Ratburn. He's one-in-a-million."

"But you were talking with Mr. Pryce-Jones about—"

"Oh, that . . ." The principal waved his hand. "The only kids Mr. Pryce-Jones will teach at Lakewood are my niece and nephew. He's going to tutor them over the summer."

Buster looked very relieved. "Well, then, HOORAY FOR ARTHUR!" he cried.

The crowd took up the cheer.

As the Lakewood kids headed for the bus, Buster told everyone else the good news about Mr. Ratburn.

"I'm glad we don't have a really tough teacher like Mr. Pryce-Jones," he said. "I'll bet he'll give those kids homework tonight."

"Homework?" said Mr. Ratburn. "Thank you for reminding me, Buster. You know, in coming here, we lost a whole day of class. We could use a little extra homework."

Everyone's face fell.

"Yes," Mr. Ratburn said. "I'd like a written report on a medieval invention by next Monday. Then perhaps a quiz on the rulers of England. And then . . ."

As Mr. Ratburn went on, Arthur pushed back the crown from his forehead. It was going to be a long week — even for royalty.